M000087344

IT HURTS
(From a Child's Perspective)

Dr. Adela Ames-Lopez

ISBN 978-1-0980-5042-9 (paperback)
ISBN 978-1-0980-5043-6 (hardcover)
ISBN 978-1-0980-5044-3 (digital)

Copyright © 2021 by Dr. Adela Ames-Lopez

All rights reserved. No part of this publication may be reproduced, distributed, or transmitted in any form or by any means, including photocopying, recording, or other electronic or mechanical methods without the prior written permission of the publisher. For permission requests, solicit the publisher via the address below.

Christian Faith Publishing, Inc.
832 Park Avenue
Meadville, PA 16335
www.christianfaithpublishing.com

Printed in the United States of America

Who Will Cry for the Little Boy?

Who will cry for the little boy?
Lost and all alone.
Who will cry for the little boy?
Abandoned without his own?
Who will cry for the little boy?
He cried himself to sleep.
Who will cry for the little boy?
He never had for keeps.
Who will cry for the little boy?
He walked the burning sand
Who will cry for the little boy?
The boy inside the man.
Who will cry for the little boy?
Who knows well hurt and pain.
Who will cry for the little boy?
He died again and again.
Who will cry for the little boy?
A good boy he tried to be.
Who will cry for the little boy?
Who cries inside of me

By Antwone Fisher

2

IT HURTS...

WHEN I CANNOT BE MYSELF!

(Please allow me to freely be who I want to be)

WHEN I AM INJURED!

(Help and support me! Please do not harm me.)

WHEN I AM LEFT ALONE!

(I need you to keep me safe. Please do not leave me
unsupervised)

WHEN I DO NOT EAT!

(I need healthy meals and snacks daily to grow up
healthy and strong.)

WHEN I AM BULLIED!

(Please appreciate and understand me for who I am!
Do not call me names or touch me and my belongings)

WHEN I STRUGGLE IN SCHOOL!

(I want to be smart and talented. Help me to find and keep my attention in school.)

WHEN MY PARENTS DO NOT TELL AND SHOW ME THAT THEY LOVE ME!

(I thrive better when you tell me and show me that
you love me. It makes me feel safe and loved.)

I DON'T WANT TO HURT ANYMORE!

(Mom and dad, when you show me love the pain goes away. Love me because I love you)

WHEN I AM HIT!

(These bruises hurt. Please do not hit me. Talk to me about what happened so I do not become a hitter like you, when I grow up.)

WHEN I DO NOT HAVE SOMEONE TO TALK TO!

(It feels better to share with a safe and trusted person.
I need you in my life.)

WHEN I AM SEPARATED FROM MY FAMILY!

(I love my family. Please help me to remain with my family, but in a safe and stable environment.)

WHEN MY PARENTS FIGHT!

(Please talk out your differences. When you hurt each other, you hurt me too!)

WHEN ME AND MY SIBLINGS FIGHT!

(Let's talk out our differences. We learn from our parents. Our bruises are reminders of our pain and how we hurt each other. I love you.)

WHEN I AM NOT HEARD!

(Please do not over talk or silence me. My voice is important. Listen to me and ask questions if you do not understand me.)

WHEN I HAVE NO WHERE TO LIVE!

(It is dangerous sleeping in cars, abandoned homes, or outside, etc. Protect me and help me to have a safe and stable place to live. I am afraid.)

WHEN I LIVE WITH STRANGERS!

(I don't know them! They don't know me! I feel uncomfortable living here. Please help me to continue living with those I know and love in a safe and stable home.)

WHEN YOU ARE ABUSING DRUGS!

(You are not yourself when you are "high". You cannot protect me. And there is a chance that I may start using drugs too. Please seek help so you can stop using drugs. I need you.)

WHEN I AM YELLED AT!

(It is embarrassing and hurtful to be yelled at. Please talk to me. It will allow me to understand and appreciate what you are saying to me. And I will learn to be a communicator rather than a yeller when I grow up.)

WHEN YOU DO NOT SMILE!

(I feel that I bring you pain when you do not smile. I feel better when you smile and share your excitement with me.)

WHEN YOU CALL ME BAD NAMES!

(I am *"insert your name here."* I am a person with a beautiful name. Please call me by my name. In doing so, it will continue to encourage and empower me.)

WHEN YOU INAPPROPRIATELY TOUCH ME!

(This is not love. This is not a secret. When I feel unsafe, I will tell a trusted person so that I can be safe and protected from you.)

WHEN YOU SHARE INAPPROPRIATE PICTURES OF ME!

(My private moments are mine and not for the world to see. Please do not share any pictures of me. And I will tell a trusted person so that I am safe and protected from you.)

I need a hug!

In memory of my grandmother, Daisy Ames

From being homeless at age seven to becoming a fighter and cancer survivor twice, she was a resilient mother, grandmother, and great-grandmother. She left behind a legacy of strength, fortitude, love, and the true essence of FAMILY! Thank you for setting the bar and showing us the true color of love, Grandmom!

About the Author

Dr. Adela Ames-Lopez, a native of Cheapside (Cape Charles), Virginia, grew up with her siblings in the Trenton, New Jersey area. Adela and her siblings enjoyed their mother's passion in helping adolescents who needed a place to stay. Her mother was a foster parent. Her mother's ministerial journey of fostering and counseling youth inspired Adela to pursue a career focusing on the safety, protection and welfare of children and youth. After twenty-five years of experience in child protection, child welfare, social services and social work/therapy, she devotes her spare time in writing children's novels.

CPSIA information can be obtained
at www.ICGtesting.com
Printed in the USA
BVHW022140280322
632722BV00017B/283

9 781098 050429